PRAISE FOR

the geography of girlhood

"**Perfectly captures** what being a teenager is all about, from the smallest insecurities to the biggest heartbreaks."
—**Sarah Dessen,**
author of *The Truth About Forever*

"Compelling, evocative, funny, sensual, and painfully real."
—**Ann Martin,**
author of Newbery Honor Book
A Corner of the Universe

"This is what it feels like to grow up, and these are the poems that every teenage girl, overwhelmed by longing, jealousy, and **passion,** would love to write."
—**Leah Stewart,**
author of *The Myth of You and Me*

"With **pithy,** evocative metaphors, Smith's free-verse poems capture the fizzy energies, soul-deadened malaises, and ultra-confident poses that mark teen girl experience.... Smith gets the climate for her geography just right."
—*Bulletin of the Center for Children's Books*

"A **beautifully written,** remarkably perceptive take on growing up. I only wish this book had been around when I was a teenager."
—**Julia Stiles**

"**Funny,** sad, all too real, and a **thorough delight** to read."
—**Tom Perrotta,**
bestselling author of *Election*

"Lyrical, gorgeous, and hard-hitting. I couldn't put it down."
—**Lauren Myracle,**
bestselling author of *ttyl*

"Kirsten Smith's verse is spare, **subtle,** and **tender.**"
—**Deb Caletti,**
author of National Book Award finalist
Honey, Baby, Sweetheart

"Alternately **caustic** and **vulnerable,** above all, Smith's writing is true."
—**E. Lockhart,** author of
The Boyfriend List

"Readers will be enormously **satisfied.**"
—*Kirkus Reviews*

the geography of girlhood

Kirsten Smith

LITTLE, BROWN AND COMPANY
New York ⌐ Boston

Little, Brown and Company

Hachette Book Group USA
1271 Avenue of the Americas, New York, NY 10020
Visit our Web site at www.lb-teens.com

First Paperback Edition: February 2007

LCCN 2005938431

ISBN 0-316-16021-0 (HC) / ISBN-10: 0-316-01735-3 (PB) / ISBN-13: 978-0-316-01735-0 (PB)

HC: 10 9 8 7 6 5 4 3 2 1
PB: 10 9 8 7 6 5 4 3 2 1

Q–FF

Printed in the United States of America

The text was set in Frutiger Light, and the display type is handlettered.

To Mel and Katie Aline
and
In memory of Stan Pollard

1

marine life

Clam season is about to start
and ninth grade is almost over
and I have rowed myself
out to the middle of the bay so I can see the place I live:
everything is trees and water and rain
and smoky stink from the paper mill
and small town, small town.

One day, I'll find my way away from here
and go somewhere real
and do something great
and be someone wonderful.
One day, I will be standing at the shore
of a completely different body of water
and it will be big and wild and dangerous
and it will be like this one
never even existed.

Fourteen

Fourteen is like rotten candy,
fourteen is a joke that no one gets.
When you're fourteen,
you look good only once a week
and it's never on the day of the dance.
When you're fourteen,
you have a mouthful of metal
that no one wants to taste.
Fourteen is going to bed at night
and wishing you could wake up with a new face
or a new dad or better yet,
a new life
that doesn't look anything
like this one.

My Sister's Body

I have been living in my sister's room
for so long,
I begin to think that
her body is mine.
The long torso,
the breasts lodged high
like tea cakes
on her powdery skin.
In our room
I watch my sister dash around,
her lips like bruised plums
as she waits for Bobby
to gun up to the house.
I look at her
and memorize everything.
So when the time comes,
and the boy's eye glitters like a crime,
I will know what to do.
I will peel off my crushed velvet shell
and stand before him,
tall and beautiful
and so white
he can barely breathe.

Pretty

They say girls take after their mothers
and in the case of my sister, it's true.

But in the case of me
I have my father's eyes and my father's toes
and scariest of all
my father's nose.

My mother was pretty
but my father is not,
so that means whatever beauty there is,
that's what my sister got.

Diana

Lips, limes, she had it all.
That's what I say about my mother,
a dreamboat that drifted away,
a flower on a live spit.
She had the beauty of a fire alarm:
loud and hard to ignore,
always too late to stop the house from burning down.
I don't remember much about her
just that she was an expert at drinking too much
and falling down just a little,
and she always said glass could cut glass,
a diamond was nothing special.

The day she left, I was six and learning to swim,
coasting like a petal in the community pool
when she came to whisper her last how-to's into
    my ear:
How to hold the man gently over the flame
until he is golden as toast,
how to butter him,
how to almost gobble him whole,
when to stop
and call him *love.*

To him, we are piles of lingerie.
We are water-rings and dented fenders,
we are a trail of CDs littering the road to nowhere.

Because of us, he's always on the prowl for chaos,
a man with a little box for this
and a little bag for that.
To him, we are the kinds of daughters that
make a man want to invent things
just so they can make their way along.

He tells us he hopes that when the time comes,
and with the help of all he's given us—
the fishing-lure markers, the toolbox,
the lectures on which boys are trouble
and which boys are good-for-nothings—
we'll be able to move gracefully
through the world.

We will be tidy and professional,
well organized and successful,
but what he doesn't know is that
we will leave just enough of a trail—
a stain on the davenport or a chip in the paint—

so that he can recognize us
as his daughters,
so he can seek us out
and call us his own.

Closet

This morning, Tara catches me.
sneaking into her closet and
when I ask to borrow one of her shirts
to wear to the dance this afternoon,
she tells me she's not loaning me anything
and if I ever go in her closet again,
she will maim me
and then kill me.
I ask her what I should wear
and she says she doesn't care
but whatever it is
it shouldn't have stripes.

Dances are a dream come true
or a nightmare,
depending on who you are
or how you talk
or what you choose to wear that day.
I made the mistake of polka dots.
I stand on the far wall
in a free-fall shame spiral.
Elaine and Denise are next to me,
hopped up on Milk Duds.
Denise is wiggling around so hard
that when Eric Chandler asks her to dance,
he can barely keep hold of her.
In his fourteenth year, Eric's arms are at war
   with his legs
and it's safe to say his legs are losing.
Then Stan Bondurant comes up
and tells a joke about Polish people
before he takes Elaine out to dance.
Stan's fine, but I have a thing about class clowns—
it seems like they'll do anything
to hide their heart.
As for me, the song is halfway over
and I am at the edge of the dance floor
like a stone at the edge of the sea,

waiting for my rough edges to be smoothed
into something worth touching,
and I tell myself that one day someone will come for me
and until then
I'll wait.

Seagulls

After the dance, I get a ride home from school
with my sister and Bobby
and they stop at the beach
to do what they do,
which means I've been sent off
to collect shells
like I'm five.
A Navy helicopter flies by
and the birds on the marsh start to panic
and the air fills with a great cloud of wings
and I realize that's how it goes here:
nothing ever happens
and if it does
all the things with wings
fly away.

Tonight after dinner, my dad shows me his new
computer program. He says it looks for signals in space
while you sleep. Are you talking about *aliens*? I ask.
He nods like it's totally normal. My father has either
officially lost his mind, or maybe he's on to something;
maybe if scientists can find life on other planets, then
maybe one day somebody can find my mother.

They say my mother was like a hydrangea,
prone to wilting and then falling apart
at the slightest sign of stress or sun.
They say my mother was a rhododendron,
she always looked better after the rain.
They say my mother did so many bad things
to so many people she loved
she was a snapdragon with nowhere to go.
Me, I say my mother was a night-blooming jasmine,
she was at her best when no one was looking.
I say my mother was a late bloomer
who didn't get time to grow,
but then again, what do I know.

It was night and the snow on the Ridge
was just starting to melt.
As they made their way up to the top
in his old truck,
my mother noticed the rams
propped against the hillside,
feeding on dirt.
The stars came out fast that night
and my mother imagined
that from somewhere on high,
someone looked down and said,
See that girl's skin? Protect it.

I was late for school today because my sister was trying to instruct me on the ways of feminine hygiene and I can't seem to get it right and tampons are officially my enemy and I will be stuck with maxi pads forever which means I will be uncool forever and it's safe to say there is definitely something wrong with me, which now makes this the fourth time today I have thought that, the other times being when Rob Calderon told me to "grow some tits" during P.E., and when I had sweat stains during third period for no reason, and when Danny Helms said that blue eyes are the prettiest and here I am, stuck with brown.

Today after I got out of play rehearsals, Skyler Reeves
came up to Denise and Elaine and me, all fresh from
cheerleading practice and wearing her shiny skirt
and her shiny hair and her shiny smile. *Can you guys
come over Saturday?* she asked and Elaine said,
Of course we can!

As Skyler walked away, Elaine was talking a mile a
minute about how cool it was going to be, and Denise
looked lost and sad and far away, and I stared at my
two best friends and saw that if we were a continent
unto ourselves, Elaine would be the north pole and
Denise would be the south and I would be somewhere
in the middle, trying to navigate all that space in
between.

We are at Skyler Reeves's house
watching Maggie Cartwright's dad's copy
    of *Showgirls*
which could be fun if it weren't so embarrassing.
Denise has spent half the night
hiding in the bathroom,
because sometimes she gets that way
around more than three people.
When I ask Elaine
if she thinks Denise is alright,
Elaine shrugs and says, *Sometimes Denise is such*
    a freak
and Skyler Reeves laughs.
Elaine acts cool and won't look at me.
But what she doesn't say
is that her half brother is in jail
and Skyler Reeves's mom is on her fifth marriage
and Maggie Cartwright likes being spanked
and I am what I am
so basically
that makes us all freaks,
doesn't it?

After the movie,
we all lay out our sleeping bags
and Skyler and Maggie start
talking about what happened
at the Senior Prom last night,
telling stories about high school girls
like Lisa Tavorino and Kelly Barnes
and Jenny Arnold and Jenny Able
as if they were movie stars.
Even my sister's name comes up once or twice
and Dinah says, *She's so pretty,* as if
I were somehow not aware of this fact.

Skyler and Elaine and Maggie are
so ready to become those girls
and then there's Denise,
who's still hiding in the bathroom,
and as for me, all I know
is that even though high school is only
three weeks and an entire summer away
it still feels like it's a faraway land of *them*
and I will forever be living
in the same old hometown of *me.*

The Jennys

The story goes that Jenny, homespun girl,
hopped onstage during the Prom last night
and started singing with the band.
Jacked-up on the fervor of fifteen,
drunk Jenny sang the girl-part of a duet,
didn't notice her boyfriend's hand
loitering on another Jenny's thigh.

High school seems filled with Jennys,
most of them hiding out as Jennifers,
others as easy-access Jens,
but these two—Jennys to the core.
They've spent the year ruling popularity contests
and baffling teachers with their identical penmanship.
They discovered beer and marijuana
and that's when the trouble started:
one Jenny liked Budweiser,
one liked smoking out on the cliff.

One Jenny has her hair tipped black,
the other wears Mike Shaw's letterman's jacket.
Last night, so the story goes, they were at the same
    dumb dance,
one Jenny onstage, the other by the lockers.
They took turns kissing the same boy:

a beer jock, more Jenny's type
than Jenny's, but it's not about the kissing anymore.
It's about the fierceness of the name,
the matching J's and A's on
every science quiz for the past eight years,
the feathered hair, the push
to get Paula off the cheerleading squad,
and the countless after-school hours spent
making high school what it is,
making sure no other Jennifer
dares to call herself Jenny again.

I come home from Skyler's to learn
that last night, after my sister's curfew
had not only been broken
but smashed into a million little pieces,
my dad went into her room
and tore down all her posters
and threw her sluttiest shoes in the trash
and drilled a lock on her door,
but he was so mad it fell off
and now there's just a hole there.

Tonight, my dad came into the living room
where I was doing everything I was supposed to do
and he said, *Penny, don't ever be like your sister*
because no good can come of it.
He told me I only had one life to live
and I'd better not ruin it
the way she was ruining hers.

Then he headed out to the garage
to hit things with other things
and I went upstairs and knelt outside my sister's door.
I looked through the little "o" my father made
and I could see Tara in there,
lying with her legs up against the wall,

scribbling in her diary
her hand speeding fast over the page,
speeding fast like the car
she drove into the ditch last fall,
scribbling down secrets
I would kill to know.

A Bunch of Stuff

As for my diary,
it's just a bunch of stuff about
how I wish certain boys would love me,
how I wish our mom hadn't left town
before we were old enough to know better,
and on and on, a bunch
of basic stupid wish lists
and lots of little secrets
that absolutely no one
would kill to know.

Basic Stupid Wish List #27

I wish I was this
I wish I was that

I wish I was thin
I wish I was fat

I wish I was Skyler
I wish I was Jean

I wish I was sexy
I wish I was mean

I wish I was beautiful
I wish I was tall

I wish Bobby loved me
but it's a pipe dream, that's all.

Hickeys

The next morning, I see what the fuss was about.
My sister's neck is covered with
a trail of dime-sized bruises,
a scrapbook of the night spent in Bobby's car
on a road so remote it's not even named
and the seats were rolled back
and the windows were fogged up
and the music was cranked
and the secrets were spilling
and it was magic,
just like how it will be
when it happens to me.

That's what Mrs. Hillstrom says to me in front of everyone in the middle of English. Two days ago, she stopped me after class to tell me that even though my grades are good, and even though she appreciates my after-school participation in *The Diary of Anne Frank,* I need to stop daydreaming about whatever I'm daydreaming about. Don't I know that this is my life? she asks me. Don't I know that I need to live in the here and now and not in a fantasy?

After Mrs. Hillstrom turns back to the board, Elaine, who's trying not to laugh, throws me a note, which hits me square in the eye.

A Note from Elaine

Penny—

Wanna hang out with me and Skyler after school today?

Xoxoxo
Elaine

P.S. Don't invite Denise.

P.P.S. Stan and I totally made out yesterday!

P.P.P.S. I heard Randall Faber might like you. Isn't that awesome?

The Note I Write Back

Elaine—

I can't hang out today cuz I have rehearsal for the play.

P.S. Why can't I invite Denise?

P.P.S. I barely even know Randall Faber.

Why do you have to go to rehearsal if you're only
   doing lighting?

P.S. Denise has gotten totally weird.

P.P.S. Stan is an awesome kisser!!!

P.P.P.S. Should I tell Randall you like him?

NO, do NOT tell Randall I like him!!!

P.S. I have to go to practice because I'm understudy for the lead, so Mrs. H says I have to be committed.

P.P.S. I don't think Denise is that weird.

Busted

Just as I throw my note to Elaine, I hear Mrs. Hillstrom
say, *Penny—detention.* I look up to see she's staring
right at me and Stan Bondurant goes, *Ooh, busted* in
this really stupid voice. He might be an Awesome Kisser
but that doesn't stop him from being a Total Ass.
Now I feel sick to my stomach because I have never
gotten detention before, but then again, to look on
the bright side, after today I will no longer be a virgin.
Of detention, that is.

Detention

Detention is nothing like a teen movie
where all the guys have Mohawks
and the girls carve hearts into their desks
and everyone is secretly smoking weed.
In my teeny tiny town
detention is a beige classroom
and a vague smell of depression
and a clock that clonks along so everyone can hear
and a bunch of people staring out the window
waiting for something to happen—
but here's the weird part—
something actually does.

Jenny Arnold's Boyfriend

A bunch of high school guys just walked by the window where I sit in detention, their lettermen's jackets glowing like blue diamonds pulled from the bottom of the bay. One of them, the one everyone knows is Jenny Arnold's boyfriend, smiled at me. When I smiled back, he put his hand to his mouth and before I knew it, Jenny Arnold's boyfriend was blowing me a kiss. I will say here and now that it was like getting an A+ in a subject I knew nothing about, or waking up with straight teeth after years of crooked ones, or winning the lottery with a ticket that just happened to be found on the ground.

Understudy

I walk out of detention dazed and in love,
rewinding and replaying over and over
my moment with Jenny Arnold's boyfriend
on the movie screen in my head.
That's what I'm doing when Denise
comes careening up and yells,
Glynis Peterson has bronchitis!
I have no idea what she's talking about
and I stand there staring at her
until she says, *Hello? The play?*
You're not the understudy anymore!
You're the star!

I.

Tonight the lead role in *The Diary of Anne Frank*
will be played by me, Penny Morrow. Tonight I am the
girl in the attic, writing it all down. All this would be
wonderful if I could remember my lines. But that is
not the case. If I were Anne Frank, history would never
have been recorded. If I were Anne Frank, history
would have been lost for good.

II.

After everyone gets their money back, Mrs. Hillstrom
tells me she's found a second understudy to take over
for the rest of my remaining performances. But what I
really wish is that she could find an understudy to take
over for the rest of my remaining life.

III.

I wait until after everyone else has left, and I walk to
the parking lot in my bad stage makeup to meet my
dad, who will most undoubtedly be late. Then, there,

in the rain that has just started to come down, is Randall Faber. In his hair is a bit of sawdust, and in his hand, a half-dozen pink carnations are glowing in their green Safeway wrapper.

IV.

I got you these _before_ I saw the show, Randall Faber says, handing me the carnations. I give him a shove and he laughs and we walk out into the rain and it's like I'm finally giving the performance I am supposed to give. Okay, I tripped once, but at least the audience is smaller.

The next day at school,
my newfound status as Screw-Up In The School Play
has been faintly dimmed thanks to
my newfound status as The Girl Randall Faber Likes.

Maggie Cartwright and Skyler Reeves
smile at me during Science
and Stan Bondurant
doesn't pick on me at recess.
Elaine wants to eat lunch with Denise and me
as if the three of us
were suddenly best friends again.

That's the upside of being The Girl Randall Faber Likes.
That's the part I can handle.
The other part is happening now,
when Elaine comes up to my locker and tells me
what will happen after the sixth period bell has rung,
what will happen when I go from being someone
used to standing on the outside of a story
to someone standing smack dab in the middle of one.

The First Kiss

The First Kiss walks on two legs
just like everyone else.
He has a birthmark and a good soccer kick.
He's first base in spring and fullback in fall,
he's too cool for hot lunch.
Today, after the bell, in front of the bus,
he's going to take me to a place I've never been.
I hear this news secondhand and third,
because, like the soldier's wife,
I am the last to know.
I am on the blade edge of the knife all day,
all I want is to stay small and young and out of the way
but here comes Elaine with lip gloss choices:
Bubble Gum, Lemon-Lime, Tutti Fruity.
She explains that this is what I am to taste like,
that the First Kiss narrowed it down from the full set
    of six.
I pick one, but all I really want
is to drop out of ninth grade and never come back.
All I want is to go somewhere where things like this
    don't happen—
kisses and the planning of them.

He holds my hand as we walk toward the bus.
From somewhere, somebody yells,
Go for it, Randall! Wooh, yeah!
and suddenly, his mouth is upon mine
and the air is reeking of Tutti Fruity,
the pineapple hitting the banana up against the cherry,
the air is smacking of fruit.

When I wake up, I'm lying on the curb.
The First Kiss has fled the scene
but the school nurse is on her way.
Elaine is patting my hand and saying,
Everything will be okay, I promise.
What she doesn't understand is that
I have really done it now,
I have really gone
and ruined my life.

You are such a retard,
my sister says when she hears what happened
because my sister is beautiful and perfect
and immune to humiliation.

I wonder if my mother
fainted after her first kiss.
Maybe it's something that I inherited from her,
maybe it's a secret only the two of us share.

My sister looks at me then smiles.
You may be an idiot,
she says before walking out of the room.
But at least you have a boyfriend now.

I do?

The Beaks and Wings of Birds

The beaks of birds
tell me what I need to know.
When my sister drives,
she tries to hit the pile of crows.
She swears they live cruel, uneven lives.
I, too, grow to hate birds
and to long for them;
their early pecking on the roof
of my house
and the puffy thump
when a sparrow hits the window.
My sister gasps,
my father barely stirs,
our dog twitches in the dull light.
I am the only one to rush outside,
because I want to see
something fallen down from flight,
I want to marvel at this
thing with wings,
I want to stand in front of
a pane of glass
and really believe
it was something I could fly through.

Going Together

I guess we are going together now,
even though technically I was never asked
to have my hand held
every single minute of the day,
I was never asked to exhaust myself
trying to make conversation
with a boy I barely know,
I was never asked to
dance with only one person
at the Friday Afternoon Dances
to songs I'm not even sure I like.
Funny how the things you ask for
you never get
and the things you don't,
you always do.

Penny has a boyfriend so you need a girlfriend,
my sister announces to my dad.
My dad stares at me and says,
What?! You have a boyfriend?!
Then my sister grins and says,
Don't worry, Dad, she's still a virgin—
but at this point
she's probably getting more action than you are.

My dad looks like he might combust or implode
like one of those planets
he studies up there in the sky.
I tell my dad he has nothing to worry about
and he says he'd better not
and then goes outside
to work on his new telescope.

My sister says the sky is full of stars
and the sea is full of fish
and maybe if he found a new one
he'd stop being so cranky
all the time.

I don't know much about stars
but maybe Tara's right.

The sky is full of them,
so why keep staring at the ones
that have spun forever
out of reach?

Caught Fish

It looks like my sister got her wish.
Dad came home the other night
smelling like beer and first date.
He'd gone to dinner with a marine biologist
    named Susan.
She counts the salmon every season,
she's the one who decides if the population is stable.
Like my sister says, there are plenty of fish in the sea
and here is a woman who knows
exactly how many.

Meatless

My father's new girlfriend is vegan
so that's why tonight
we're having squash and stir-fry for dinner.
My father used to be a man who loved meat
but now it seems he's lost his taste for flesh.
Susan says that's how they met.
It was at a barbecue at the Snyders';
he asked her what a tofu dog tasted like
and she said, *Here, try a bite of mine,*
and he did.
My sister and I look at each other.
This does not sound like our father,
a man who doesn't like new food
or new people or new anything,
and yet there he was,
eating some meatless wiener
out of the palm
of a strange woman's hand.

There's only one more week left of junior high, but I am treasuring each moment of it because every day between 2:10 and 2:17 Jenny Arnold's boyfriend walks by my sixth period science class. Every day between 2:10 and 2:17, Jenny Arnold's boyfriend looks at me, or winks, or smiles, or stares, or waves at me through the window and it feels like my body is being hijacked by the ocean or the wind or a lightning storm and I wonder, Can you love someone if you've never spoken to them? Can someone be telling you they love you just by looking at you? I don't know what love is, but if it's anything less than this, how could it possibly matter?

Things They Say About Love

When I break up with Randall,
everyone wants to know why
I'd do something so dumb.

What I want to know is,
haven't they ever heard a song
or read a poem or watched a movie?

If they had, they'd know
that love is a school
where the only curriculum is kissing,
love is the first day of sun
after a whole winter of rain,
love is a secret thicket of small trees
just outside of town,
love is how you are born,
love is how you ruin your life.

So when people ask, I want to tell them
that whatever this was,
it definitely wasn't that.

If there was a list of stupid things to do, flirting with Jenny Arnold's boyfriend would be smack-dab at the tippy-top. Denise tells you the word is out: Jenny Arnold is going to kill you the day you hit high school. She tells you that Jenny Arnold says this summer is your last, so you'd better enjoy it.

The next time you see Jenny Arnold's boyfriend, he doesn't look at you. You stare at him through the window of junior high, the one that looks out on the rest of your life, and you realize this is the first boy you're going to die for, and if you live through the summer, it probably won't be the last.

2

low tide

It's the first day of summer and
the sun rises like a giant, dumb saucer.
I take the dogs and
sit outside in the gory heat,
waiting for Tara to come home
and face all the trouble that can't help
but flare up around her.
She's been out all night
and I try to picture what she was doing and with whom,
but it's about as easy as trying to picture
dying or being born.

The heat is starting to slap me around now
and after I fill the dog dishes with water,
I sit there and wonder
if there will ever be a mystery inside of me
like there is inside my sister—
something bright and fast and wonderful,
something awful and true, something
that cannot be stamped out
no matter how many ways
our father tries to stamp it out.

Summer has lost all control of itself
when Tara's car pulls in the drive.

Our father waits at the door for her,
fighting the heat.
My sister gets out and gives me a little wave
before she goes to face him,
and I sit there,
waiting for the noise to start,
watching as the dogs run wild around the yard,
eating things that will make them sick later,
bringing back things the rest of us thought
were long since buried and gone.

Visiting South

Every July my sister goes
to be a camp counselor
and I get sent south,
away from the sea and the pines
and to the flat land of boy cousins
and tumbleweeds.

Even though we're too old for it,
the boy cousins and I play marbles all summer long,
the banter of glass globes
in the lap of my summer dresses.
Always, the sex of cousins smells sharper
than that of the boys back home,
especially this summer,
the summer before high school,
with the liquid flood of marbles all around,
the print of lineoleum on my cheek,
the beer bread crumbs
dug in my knees.

This must be the start of the sweet and hungry days,
out here in the overgrown acres of forever
with the boy cousins,
because I feel like soon I will taste sin firsthand

and maybe even the way I smile, or walk,
even the way I roll the marbles
across that endless floor,
will surely give me away.

The Postcard I Imagine My Sister Writes from Camp

There's a guy here who looks just like you, Bobby.
He's got sideburns and a sunburn. He's a loser and a
sycophant. Trouble is, he says the most beautiful things,
walks the most beautiful walk. First day I saw him,
I thought, *There he is, the fool I'll fall for.* He calls
Tamakwa "summer camp for the hormonally insane."
He thinks he's clever and oh my God, he is. He's not
wasteful like you are, he doesn't waste my time with
stories about cousins or killers. The stories he tells, they
get right to the point, like a dog's nose to a crotch.
Your stories never had much of a point and if they did,
I never understand how you got to it. This guy, he's
special in a stupid kind of way. He knows how not
to hurt me, he knows how to bring up his girlfriend
casually in conversation, he knows better than to lay
himself in front of me and hold out a hand that could
mean either "Stop" or "Come Closer."

Wedding Day

My sister and I come home to find
that our father has spawned with Susan,
his bride-to-be that wants to get married at sea.
I'm in the catch and release program,
she likes to say, thinking it's funny
that she's had more boyfriends
than there are salmon in the jetty these days.

As we're motoring out to the harbor,
I look at my father, cheeks flushed,
new wedding ring burning a hole in his pocket.
As he steers us across the shallow part of the shoal,
I try not to think of my mother,
instead I look at my sister,
who's wearing Bobby's leather jacket
and not even trying to hide her latest hickey,
and Susan, the brand-new bride
who is tagging my father with a kiss and a vow
before one day she releases him
back into the wild.

Stepbrother

One day he was a kid three grades below me,
and the next we're related.
He's more disgusting than the parts of a fish
you throw in the trash.
Fortunately, he doesn't say much to me,
except for *pass that* at the dinner table
or *are you finished?* when referring to the bathroom
or food of yours he wants to eat.
He's always down at the docks,
collecting marine life, the kind that stinks when it dies.
His glasses are big like goggles
and for a person I'd prefer knowing nothing about,
why do I have to accidentally see him naked at least
    once a month?
His mother is always saying how
he needs a positive male role model
and I agree.
He's in desperate need of a dad
but one thing's for sure:
he's not getting mine.

Randall Faber called me today to wish me a happy
birthday and I said *thank you* and he asked me *what'd
you do?* and I told him *I went to North Carolina to see
my relatives and when I got back I had a whole new
family.* Actually, I didn't say that last part.

Randall told me he spent his summer building an
add-on to his kitchen with his dad and his brothers.
Also, he got a new dog.

I picture the Faber family—a gang of boys and a mom
that makes the meals and a dinner table full of people
that know how to love each other in a regular way.
It sounds nice, I say, and Randall says it is, and he
asks how Elaine is and I say we're not really friends
anymore, and he asks how Denise is, and I say I'd
rather not talk about it and then we say goodbye,
and that's it.

Denise is sick in the head
and has been since June,
when she killed something for the first time.
Her father gave her traps for the kitchen and den
and orchestrated their placement,
as if he were back in Da Nang,
festooning the forest with a collar of landmines.

I was sleeping over
the night he gave out the orders,
and in the morning, we collected the bodies
and bagged them before breakfast—
three rigid mice and one warm one,
soft and barely bleeding,
fresh from the thunder of running from cats.

We took them out to the trash
and there, under the rotting elm,
Denise's sobs were the sound of a prom dress
being taken off in a parking lot—
slick and satiny and torn.
Her father, all bourbon eyes and confiscated heart,
didn't like tears
and refused us food
until they were dry and gone.

Now, Denise can't wait to kill things.
Last week, slain beasts were taking the form of
cats and squirrels, then birds and bees,
and now she's got her sights on
boys from the neighborhood and beyond,
some of them so big they could only be called men.
She's ready for them all to fall down, one by one,
until the town is littered with creatures
whose hearts she's broken,
with me, faithful witness, following just behind,
tagging the bodies
so the next of kin
can always be notified.

Today is my fifteenth birthday
so Tara is playing the part of Perfect Sister,
beautiful on the half-shell,
experienced but never vampy.
Oh, I know, she has her problems:
the way she couldn't stop knitting
that scarf for Susan for Christmas
(it just grew and grew, an avenue of red yarn),
the broken curfews, the pregnancy scare,
the tendency to do everything
everyone tells her *not* to do.

But all in all, she's a pretty picture,
teeth white as the sky,
eyes marshy and green as Florida.
With her lipstick that matches the moon,
she's telling loaves of lies,
saying she never starts fights,
saying she's gained weight, really she has.
She goes on and on,
sipping from a bottle of something
swiped from the berth below
and leaning against me in quieter moments,
whispering *I love you* as we round the point,

just before Dad drops the mainsail
and with the sure hand of a father,
takes us back to shore.

Favorite Foods

When we get home from our sail,
all sunburned and salty,
I walk into my room
and find a boy I barely know
reading my diary.
He's got it open to my list of Favorite Foods
(I told you my diary was stupid)
and I scream *What are you doing?!*
My stepbrother leaps up and runs out
and I slam the door in his face
and after a moment I hear him say,
I like tacos, too.
But when I open the door, he's gone.

Don't tell Elaine, Denise says
when she shows me the medication the doctor
   put her on.

Don't tell Denise, Elaine says
during the only phone call we have all summer,
the one where she brags about having sex with
   Stan Bondurant.

Don't tell my mom, my stepbrother says
after I catch him feeding a stray cat
outside our house.

I'm usually not a person people trust with their secrets
but in two weeks school starts
and it's obvious to everyone that after that,
the only place I'll be taking those secrets
is to the grave.

Labor Day

The harbor is alive with motors
and the sun is shining or something like it
and the Sound is full of jellyfish
and the gulls are flirting with their catch
before they come to kill it.
I am down at the dock
trying with all my might
to stop summer from ending
and so is Larry in slip 15
who's had enough of his life
so he just drinks his way through it,
or the guy who lives on the tugboat
that my stepmom says might sink,
but no matter what, the spangle and spell of school
is coming for me like a tide I can't stop,
it's coming for me like a storm off the coast,
it's coming for me like a spark that sets the
   forest aflame
and while all the girls are like bulbs about to bloom,
me, I am trying to stay dug down in the dirt
because I know what is waiting for me
when I come out.

3

the lay
of the land

Don't ask me why, but
I've decided that being afraid of Jenny Arnold
is more powerful than being in love.
Love isn't five feet nine like Jenny Arnold is.
Love doesn't drive a lime green Barracuda the way
    Jenny Arnold does.
And love won't kill you like Jenny Arnold will.

On the drive to school, I ask my sister
if she'll protect me from what's about to happen.
My sister just laughs.
She can't wait for me to die so she can get my room.
When we get to school,
everyone is having the time of their goddamn lives
and all I can think about is my funeral.

I'm on my way into second period gym
and that's when I see Jenny Arnold
standing in the locker room,
wearing nothing but her underwear and a rose tattoo
    on her hip—
a thorny invitation to sniff
and get pricked.
Jenny Arnold doesn't care who sees her and why
    should she?

She's a rock star in a room full of doofs,
she's done things the rest of us have never even
    read about.
She walks towards me, topless and queenly and
I realize I've been dreaming about getting hit by
    Jenny Arnold
all summer long, the way some girls dream about
    getting kissed.
Suddenly, I can't wait for the punch;
at least I'm going to die at the hand
of someone who's beautiful and cool.

I close my eyes and wait
to get smacked, but instead
Jenny Arnold smiles and says,
Welcome to high school
and then she walks away,
heading toward the showers
like a flower blooming towards the rain
and for no reason at all,
I go from feeling cursed to blessed,
because like any goddess on high,
Jenny Arnold has the gift of taking life
and she has the gift of giving it back.

Just Friends

Why I have to have a locker right next to Randall Faber,
I will never know.
Every day I see him and we pretend like it's normal
like we're "just friends"
except inside I feel kind of sick,
knowing that no matter how old I get,
Randall Faber will always be my first kiss,
my first beginning, my first end.
I guess the upside is that
now I'm a woman with a past,
I'm not all present and future like I used to be
and maybe that's a good thing
if it weren't so absolutely awful.

Some people are only happy if they are making your life miserable and Mr. Horter is one of them. He enjoys the torture of frogs and freshmen. His life is sure to be awful, because his head is pointy and he is cruel and his pants are weird. He is destined to a life with a wife who (I've seen her) is as mean as he is. I imagine them kissing each other at the door when he comes home. Then I try to imagine him getting her pregnant (which she is) and all I can imagine is two people bumping up against each other in a pitch-black room. I don't know what my life holds, but if it's anything like Mr. Horter's, I don't want it. What I'd like to know is, shouldn't they have teachers that inspire you to grow up, instead of people whose lives seem to say, *Stop now because it's never going to get any better*?

Erosion

Denise and Elaine don't talk at all anymore.
They are like that cliff in town,
the one that's sliding into the sea.

Geologists say the erosion was inevitable.
Nothing could stop it,
not with the rain and the wind the way it is.

Whether it's soil or best friends,
things can't help but slip away and disappear.
I guess nothing on the map ever stays fixed.
All you can do is make sure you're not standing on it
when it goes.

My Mother at Fifteen

I don't know much about my mother, just that she had wanderlust all her life, even at fifteen, with her lipstick and her too-short skirt and her foster parents yelling at her from the house. My mother was a person who always wanted to leave wherever she was.

She told me once that her first kiss was with a traveling salesman. She told me once that she left home at sixteen. She told me once that I was just like her.

The Valley

After the first semester of tenth grade
is over, I ride my bicycle
into Anderson Valley.
I've never been down here before
and there's something faraway about it,
the way it's overgrown with cows and plum trees
and the distant cat calls of dogs and birds.

I guess the thing I never imagined about high school
is how suddenly there would be a whole landscape
    of boys
and it's not like I get to take my pick or anything,
but I can be in love with whomever I want,
I could love someone who's two years older
or six inches taller,
I could love someone who hunts
or someone who fishes,
or someone who doesn't believe in either.

The rain is starting now and
I pedal further into the valley,
no idea where I'm going
except knowing that when I get there
I'm going to realize
just how lost I really am.

Motorbike

I pedal home, following the smell of motorbike.
Bobby just bought one, so my sister
has spent the week with her arms
wrapped around his waist
racing through alleys and other parts unknown.
My sister is sparkly with friends and people that
    love her,
my sister is a walking tiara.
She is everyone's prize
but the only thing she seems to want
is the smell of gasoline in her hair
and the taste of something
that doesn't taste like anything else
on her lips.

After a dinner of succotash stew
my stepmother does dishes
and my father looks at our report cards.
He tells Tara just because she's in love
it doesn't mean now she can flunk all her classes.
He tells me that just because I get A's in English
it doesn't mean I can get C's in every other subject.
He tells my stepbrother *Good job*
because he gets straight A's in everything.
That's probably because he has no life,
my sister says and I laugh.
Our stepmother gives us one of her vegan glares
because her son is the model of perfection
and we are just the messes
she's being forced to clean up.

On Fire

I think the only reason Denise started smoking is
because she likes to see things burn. I'm starting to
think she likes lit matches more than being my friend.
I guess it makes sense; she's always lived her life like it's
going up in flames any second. One day, she's going to
start a fire and she's not going to be able to stop it.
One day she's going to start a fire and I won't have the
water to put it out.

History Class

As for my other (so-called) friends,
Elaine and Skyler walked into history class today
with Charlotte Ames and some other girls
and they were all waving their pom-poms around
and squealing about the game tomorrow
and I wanted to throw up on their shoes
until Mr. Stearns said,
For those of us who aren't sports fans,
can you keep it to yourselves?
I loved him for that.
And have you ever noticed what
nice hands he has?

The Bus

Charlotte Ames rides my bus
and she's the kind of girl who's born happy.
She is sunny and bright and pure,
she doesn't have crazy thoughts
passed down to her by a mother
who left town before she knew how to count.
Her parents are PTA All The Way.
When it comes to crazy,
I am definitely a "have"
and she is a "have-not."

Except this morning, Charlotte Ames
gets on the bus and she can't stop crying
and she tries to hide it
but it's like a thunderstorm is raging
inside her pep squad uniform.
She sits down next to me and
I pretend not to notice the typhoon of her sadness
is gaining speed and velocity.
Soon, cars and homes will be in danger.
Soon, there will be mandatory evacuations.

I know nothing about Charlotte Ames
But I know what it means to be that sad
and how sometimes sadness is the loneliest kind
    of bad weather,
it's more like lightning than rain
because it only strikes a person who least suspects it.
But I don't say this to Charlotte Ames.
Instead I just hand her the napkin from my bag lunch
and she mops her face and
we ride the bus together to school
without speaking, the two of us floating down a river
whose banks have long since flooded.

The Big Game

Tonight is the night
of the big game
and it's so dumb
people call it that
because it seems like
it's the same size
as any other old game.

Quarterback

I do not want to love you
because that's everyone else's job.
It's the job of Elaine and Dawn,
of Skyler and Maggie and Charlotte,
girls I've grown up with,
girls who line the field at night
to watch you sprint and score,
your face a never-ending flush of tiny victories.

I do not want to love you
because I fall to ruin watching you
run and sprint and lob things
into the air so high
they might never come down.

I do not want to think about you
walking towards me or
taking me to places I have never been.
I do not want to think about you
at night, when no one is thinking of me.
I do not want to love you,
so I am giving you to the other girls;
they can have you and the sun that smiles down on you,
they can have you and the sky that opens up for you,
they can have you
and they can keep you.

Geometry

In that "I hate my life" voice of hers,
Mrs. Shields is going on and on
about polygons and parallel lines
when somebody pokes me on the back.
It's Jenny Arnold, passing me a note.
I open it, thinking it might be from Denise
but I don't get many notes from Denise
because she barely comes to school anymore.

Instead it's in Jenny's famous handwriting:
Where'd you get those shoes?
They're vintage, I write back,
which is sort of true
because technically they are secondhand,
having been stolen from my sister's closet
just this morning.
Jenny writes back, *Cool*
which is practically like getting a note from God
telling you you're getting into heaven.

If that weren't enough, she writes back:
What kind of music do you like?
The usual stuff, I write and she writes back,
Then obviously you need my help.

She gives me a grin
and suddenly, I love quadrilaterals
and supplementary angles
and I love geometry
because Jenny Arnold
just became my friend.

1. Rebel Girl—Bikini Kill
2. Violet—Hole
3. Fuck and Run—Liz Phair
4. I Know I Know I Know—Tegan and Sara
5. Portions for Foxes—Rilo Kiley
6. This Isn't It—Lemona
7. Oh!—The Breeders
8. One More Hour—Sleater Kinney
9. Y Control—Yeah Yeah Yeahs
10. Dress—PJ Harvey
11. Dirty Knives—The Bangs
12. Gigantic—Pixies
13. The Difference Between Love and Hell—
    Sahara Hotnights
14. Yes She Is My Skinhead Girl—Unrest
15. Bull in the Heather—Sonic Youth
16. Summer Babe—Pavement
17. I Am a Scientist—Guided By Voices
18. The Falls—French Kicks
19. The Tide That Never Came Back—The Veils
20. Maybe Not—Cat Power

Spaz

My stepbrother comes into my room
reeking of spaghetti and video games.
What are you listening to? he asks.
A mix CD. I shrug.
Who's on it?
You wouldn't know the bands, I say.
And he says, *Maybe I should make a mix CD for
    Beth Sczepanick.*
I ask him who Beth Sczepanick is
and he says, all blushing and dorky, *She's this girl.*
Then he blurts, *She's really good at ice-skating!*
I stare at him.
Are you in love?
Instead of answering,
he runs out of the room,
tripping over a pair of shoes
and then spastically falling down in the hallway
which is further proof that he just might be
the most ridiculous person
I have ever met.

You're the girl my stepbrother's in love with
and he's just the twelve-year-old kid
of a lady my dad married last year.

It's not like I care about him,
in fact, he drives me crazy
with his stories about you,
the figure skater who's skated
a perfect flower on the rink of his heart.
He won't shut up about your double axels
and your triple-toe loops
and how once you smiled at him in the hall.

Personally, I suspect you've never even noticed him
and why should you?
He's not much to look at
but he's got shiny hair and
sometimes he smells like cinnamon
and yesterday, he went to the mall
and bought me a pair of really ugly earrings
that are kind of cute.

Which is why I'm telling you now
that if you hurt him, or carve a figure eight
into one of his soft spots,

I will fill your locker with hate notes,
I'll carve *bitch* into the side of your sled.
I'm not above snagging your tutu
and tampering with your blades,
breaking bones or poisoning your cocoa,
because this good boy with a broken heart
is like you without ice to skate on.

These sound like pale threats, but trust me,
if you hurt this dumb-ass kid
I never thought I'd know,
your life will be spent
in the hot nub of a sunny day,
waiting at the edge of a lake
that just won't freeze over.

The Last Day of Tenth Grade

It's the last day of tenth grade
and all I have to show for it
are a bunch of B plusses
a very strange stepbrother
a very vegan stepmother
one ex-friend that's ditched me
to become a cheerleader
another friend who's going as crazy as her father is
a sister who hates me
a never-ending crush on her boyfriend—
but the weirdest part
is that I am leaving tenth grade
being friends with the girl
who was the whole reason
I didn't want to show up in the first place.
If anyone tells you that life is predictable,
DO NOT BELIEVE THEM.

4

Bodies of Water

Permission

I've never asked my father to stay out late before.
Because of this, he interrogates me for an hour like
I'm one of the guys who work for him at the mill.
Where are you going and *When will you be back* and
Are you sure you'll be back and it goes on and on, until
finally my stepmother says, *Gerald, it's fine. It's summer
vacation. Let her go.* Then she smiles at me and it
makes her look kind of pretty and for the first time,
I can sort of see why my father fell in love with her.

We leave twenty bucks in an envelope
and get our bottle of whatever
from a tire in Mike Neeson's front yard
because he is legal
and we are not.

We go to the drive-in to drink it
and it tastes terrible but Jenny says that's not the point,
it's about the way it makes you feel.
I feel dizzy and dangerous
and temptation sits like a pat of yeast
on my tongue, rising and rising
and sour.

It's dusk when the movie starts
to filter through the trees
and Jenny says, *Come on,*
let's go downtown,
and she starts the car and we drive away
heading for trouble
like we're heroines in the making
like we're starlets getting lit into being
by the curving screen.

Jenny sneaks into the Hilltop
and smuggles me out a beer
before going back in.
A drunk guy's outside
telling a really loud story about
a fight he got into last week
with his neighbor
and then I turn around
and there's Mr. Stearns,
my history teacher.
He laughs and says, *I'm not going to ask*
what you're doing here, Penny.
and I say, *Then I guess I'll have to ask you*
what you're doing here
and he kind of laughs
and that's how it started.

I want to know what it's like
to fall against you in the heat,
you, my own history teacher,
my own Battle of Gettysburg,
my thirteen colonies.
You have hiked from here to Idaho and back,
always loving the wrong woman,
the compass biting your palm,
your sex swaying like a bean stalk.
It's as though you'll always
be a teenager, a scalding runt,
self-centered, effusive, your
crooked teeth like Letters of Congress,
like crates of tea in the Boston Habor.

Tonight, as we stand outside the Hilltop Tavern,
my B's and B plusses glittering behind us
and Jenny yelling *Come on!* from the car,
I want to know what its like.
With this liquor quick around my hips,
state capitols slurring my speech,
I want to see whole declarations of independence
float from between your lips,
and I want to believe
they are meant just for me.

Anything

Were you flirting with <u>Mr. Stearns</u>?!
Jenny yells when I get in the car
and we laugh and laugh and
all I know is
at this moment I feel like
I can do anything I want
and be anyone I want
and go anywhere on the globe
and still call it home.

Party at Rick Stangle's

By the time we get to Rick Stangle's
famous Start of Summer party
it's almost eleven.
After everything that's happened tonight
I've almost forgotten
this is the first actual "party"
I've ever been to.
But when I get there I realize
that parties are basically just
School With Booze.
All the same people are here
wearing all the same clothes
talking about all the same things,
except they are having fun
and people who would never normally
converse with each other
are drunk enough to actually do it
and there's something
sort of sweet about it
even though from what I can tell,
it does seem to involve
a lot of vomiting.

Moonlight

I walk out into the moonlight
and there in Rick Stangle's backyard
are my sister and Bobby
and I stop and stare
because when it comes to them,
I can never stop looking.
Watching them is like a disease
I can't be cured of.

Tonight, though, instead of pulling Bobby
into her arms like she always does
my sister shoves him away
as if something has unhinged in her.
Then Jeff Eckman, who has slept with everything
    that moves
calls over, *Come here, Tara,* and
without a second thought,
my sister goes.

Bobby stands there in the moonlight,
jamming his hands in his pockets
and for the first time
he looks like someone gentle and sweet
like someone I might know
or someone I might be.

Covering

My sister crawls in through her window
at three in the morning,
and I'm there waiting,
having already covered for her
and been yelled at by Dad
for being half an hour late.
Were you with Jeff Eckman? I ask
And she says, *So what if I was?*
I glare at her.
Bobby loves you.
Bobby is an idiot, she says.
No, he isn't!
If he's so great, why don't <u>you</u> go out with him,
    she mutters
and crawls into bed
pulling the covers up over her
lying, cheating, beautiful head.

Doctor's Visit

I haven't seen Denise all summer,
until today, when she came over
after her doctor's visit.
When I asked her how it went
she said she told the nurse,
I feel restless, I forget street names,
my house key has been missing for days.

Remove your clothes,
the nurse replied,
and stand against the wall.
Pretend you are in your own house
or better yet pretend
your name means desire
in a different language.

The form they gave Denise was standard:
Chicken pox? *Yes,* she wrote, *only last year,*
contracted from the children's section
of the public library.
Herpes? *He was a brave man,* she said,
his room was filled with war medals.
Alcoholism? *Well, there is*
a bottle beside my bed
but I don't remember how it got there.

As for the doctor,
he had her lie on a table.
She said her body was remarkably quiet
as she recalled scenes from *The Wizard of Oz.*

I felt tears clotting my eyes
and I pulled her to me,
my faraway friend
who said she could still feel the stethoscope cool
    against her heart,
who said she could still smell the cool paper
    beneath her,
who said she knew that
if she wished hard enough
she could make herself well.

For my sixteenth birthday, Jenny says I need to forget about the fact that Denise won't come out of her room. Jenny says I need to forget about everything and go a rock show. Jenny says I owe myself a good time. *When have you ever done anything crazy on your birthday?*

She's right: last birthday, I went sailing. The one before that, I went to a fancy dinner at a stuffy restaurant with my dad. Of all of them, I remember my fourth birthday the best. I ate cake and my mother gave me a globe. She held it and said, *Where should we go?* I shrugged. *I don't know.* She spun the globe, then stopped it with a finger. *Wherever I'm touching, that's where we go,* she said, lifting her finger off Mozambique. *See? We've got a whole world to choose from,* she said. Later, as she was tucking me into bed, she put the globe on my dresser. *If you ever need me,* she smiled, *just remember I'll always be somewhere on here.* And two weeks later, she was gone.

As the ferry coasts into downtown,
all lit up and windy and magic,
I realize kids who grow up in cities
must never dream of
going anywhere else
because they're already there.

A Date with the Night

Here we are, sixty miles from home,
standing in a club
with the coolest people on the planet
who can probably tell we're from
the uncoolest place on the planet.

Jenny says we have to get closer to the stage
so we push our way to the front
where kids are sitting on the ground
and some of them are sneaking smokes
and wearing Yeah Yeah Yeahs T-shirts
and Jenny's got a flask of something
and then the lights dim
and everyone screams
and the first chord is struck
and the lead singer runs onstage
wearing something
she starts to rip herself out of
and people are shoving and squishing
and I am in the middle of it all,
hot and breathless and happy,
like it was someplace
I was born to be.

One Day

When I get home from the concert
at two in the morning,
Spencer is sitting in the living room
reading *Lord of the Rings*
for the umpteenth time.
Don't ask me how I got stuck with
the world's biggest nerd
waiting up for me,
but there you go.
To make matters worse, he says,
maybe one day I'll go to concerts, too
and he looks at me with this dorky look
as if I'm Arwen the Elf Queen
instead of just me.

Legal Now

Today I got a 96 on my driver's test
which means I am as close to free
as being sixteen can be.
I am four tires and a miniskirt,
I am heaven on wheels.
According to the guy from the DMV,
I got the highest score
of any girl this summer.
He said, statistically, women
score at least 75% lower than men do
and I said, that must be one good thing
about being left with a dad
and not a mom.

Dial Tone

Bobby calls our house tonight
to talk to Tara
and I can't bring myself to tell him
she's out with Jeff Eckman
so I lie and say
she's at a movie with Lisa Tavorino.
I ask if I can take a message
and he says *No,*
but you have a good night, Penny.
I sit there for a few minutes
listening to the dial tone
like it's music or something
because that's the first time
he's ever said my name.

Rainstorm

The summer ended with a rainstorm,
the only rain August had seen in years.
It came down strange and sudden
as if to remind us
we may think we know
what's going to happen
but we don't.

Live Wire

While I was inside safe and warm,
Randall Faber went out
into the summer storm
with his brothers and his father.

While I was inside, safe and warm,
that's when Randall Faber's hand
first touched the live wire.

I imagine that was the moment
when everything went gold,
sonnets loosening in his cheeks,
the universe uncaged like a pack of stars,
the molecules sloping through him,
his mouth opening as if ripening for a kiss
and that small *ah* escaping into the rain,
the three men watching their fourth
fall to the damp ground,
platter of leaves and shoes,
watching as their boy falls upon it,
his body a heave of light.

5

the
river of sixteen

Who Loved Randall the Most

At school, there's an unspoken contest
to see who loved Randall the most.
The results are based on things like
the amount of Loud Sobs Emitted During Third Period
or Handwritten Notes From Randall In Your Possession.

So far, his ex-girlfriend Janelle
seems to be gaining the edge
on his current girlfriend Tammy,
simply based on the sheer number of
Items of Clothing Received.

Tammy started dating Randall this summer
so she didn't have time
to collect his letterman's jacket
or his track jersey or his used wristbands,
two of which yesterday
Janelle wore simultaneously.

As for me, people barely remember
those few weeks in junior high
when I belonged to Randall Faber,
making this a contest I don't care to enter
because all I have to show

is a sloppy old first kiss
and the ratty memory of a dead boy's hand
that somehow found its way
into mine
and then out again.

Pop. 9,761

In big cities, kids die all the time
so when someone dies in a small town,
statistically speaking,
it's like you lose
25 people
all at once.

At Randall's funeral,
Elaine talks to me for the first time in a year.

By the bathroom, I see Stan Bondurant
and Pete Larson, who last week
were almost in a fistfight,
and now they're locked in a hug.

Fullbacks are crying by a spate of orchids,
girls who hate each other are holding hands.

Tennis players are sitting next to punk rockers,
band nerds and brainiacs are in the same pew
as cheerleaders and art freaks.

Jenny for the first time in a long time doesn't make fun
    of anybody.
Denise for the first time in three weeks comes out of
    her room.

Elaine says, *I'm sorry,* and hugs me
and I don't know if it's about Randall or for the year
we've spent apart, but it doesn't matter.

I don't know how to put it other than
everything is turned upside now,
like a crab on its back
that can't get upright again.

Losing You

Look what losing you has done to us.
The student body president doesn't even bother
to give a speech on the first day of school.
A month later, the town slut gets voted
    homecoming queen.
All the boys who were your friends
lose every bit of promise they have
to the bottle or bad grades.

You are in the ground now
and I stand at the Kanouk Island bridge,
fishing for something I'll never catch
reeling in nothing but moss
losing nothing but time
my hook coming up empty
over and over again.

Sleeping Bag

Do you ever think of us here on Earth,
wishing you back,
turning to drug or drink?
Do you ever come back to spy on us?
Nights like this one, I spend the night
in the yard, looking at the stars and wondering
Are you somewhere up there in all that?

On the day of your funeral,
your mother handed out 4x6
copies of your school photo
and then we never saw her again.
Wherever she lives now,
it's a place that never stops being night.

Me, I'm giving myself over to a foggy fiction,
photo in a yearbook,
sweet remnant of a kiss I'll never have again.
In the end, I'm just a girl
on a sleeping bag in the middle of nowhere,
at the starting line of every mistake
she'll ever make.

The Petty Thief

Lately, I've been having dreams about stealing
so I decide what's the difference
between dreaming it and doing it.
At the market, at the drugstore,
I take lipsticks, hard candy like the kind
in Grandpa's dish, items small as bones.
The stolen lipstick looks perfect on my mouth
and I know that stealing
does not make me an evil person.
In fact, the easy fever
that comes when I step outside
makes me feel beautiful, ripe and waxy,
crazy for a man to come
sweeping along, fresh from prison,
and show me all that crime can be.
The bother and the guns,
the smell of urine in the front parlor.
With my pocketful of loot,
I traverse the halls
like some kind of starlet.
I eye the boys and the girls at school
and wonder if any of them
are living out their dreams
like I am.

The Urge

God, you're depressing, my sister tells me as we're
   driving to school.

You really should snap out of it, Jenny says in the
   library one day
before leaving to go talk to Jenny Able.

Denise would probably tell me the same things
but she's busy sneaking cigarettes with the burnouts
   out back.

Are you always going to be this sad? my stepbrother
   asks.

All I know is that
the urge to run or kiss or steal or fight
is coming faster now, and maybe
my mother was right,
maybe the only place to go
is away.

You are the ex-boyfriend of my sister
a girl I'm not even sure I care about,
let alone love.
I am the girl who was always in her room,
lips sweating at the thought
of your police record.
Tonight, you show up at our house
and my sister is nowhere in sight.
I am a bungle of hubcaps on a hot day
waiting for someone to drive me off the lot.
Could I get a ride? I ask
and you open your car door for me.
All I want is for some of your bad boy
to rub off on my hands like newsprint.
As your blue-jeaned leg
whispers against mine,
the smell of grade school,
of paste and geography texts,
rises around us,
like the smell of something
already long gone,
like some powder
dropped on the ordinary world.

Everywhere

In Bobby's car,
I feel like I'm a cork about to pop.

Bobby says, *Where do you want to go?*
and I shrug and say, *Anywhere.*

What I really want to say is,
Take me everywhere you took Tara
and do everything you did to her
and say everything you said.

What I really want to say is,
Show me what it was like
so I could know now
what I could only guess at
back then.

The Marina

Bobby smells like beer and wood chips
and as we walk down the dock
he takes my hand
and a hot flash of happiness hits me.
The boats heave and squeak around us
and the moon sits fat and bright above us
as if from somewhere across the sky
the sun is sending it a kiss
full on the mouth.

Where Have You Been?

My stepmother asks me when I got home
and I say *nowhere.*
My sister looks at me funny.
She's been with a guy, she says.
What guy? My dad sits up straight.
My stepbrother looks like he wants to leave the room.
I haven't been anywhere, I lie.
After dinner, my sister stops me in the hall
and says, *C'mon, who were you with?*
You wouldn't want to know, I say
because if anything is the truth,
that is.

Mementos

My stepbrother is telling me
how he danced with Beth Sczepanick
at the Friday Afternoon Dance
and he goes on and on
about what he said
and what she said
and what he did
and what she did.

It's only been two years
since I was at that very same dance
but when I think of those days
they feel like snapshots
from the story
of someone else's life.

Typical Bobby

It was typical Bobby, typical me:
typical of him to call me into his garage,
typical of me to follow.
I was sixteen, hoping for a kiss
or a jar of his mom's peaches.
Little did I know I'd be greeted
with a freshly skinned half-buck,
another one of Bobby's prize marks.
Red and helpless, it swung there
as Bobby showed me around
the circumference of the body,
showed me the parts his mother
would make into a meal.

Never much of a braggart,
Bobby didn't put the deer's horns
on his roll-bar the way Stan Bondurant does.
And he hasn't told many
about last night in the woods
when I scampered into his camper
and ended up staying there,
giving him things he was used to hunting for
but never catching.

Be it in the slow dance or the forest,
Bobby likes to have flesh here and there.
He likes bringing me into his garage
and kissing me beside the kill.
Give him an animal without its skin,
or me without my underwear,
and you'd have typical Bobby:
his left hand resting on the flanks,
his right not pausing until
it was inside the body,
until it had found for certain
the meaning of tender.

Meteor Shower

Tonight, my dad calls me outside.
At first I think he's found out
where I was last night
or what I did,
but all he wants to say is that
tonight there's a meteor shower,
big bath of stars
that comes once a century.
I knock out a laugh of relief
and we stand under the night sky
which seems to be falling to pieces all around us.
He pulls me close and says *my little girl*
and for a moment
it's as if he knows
that I'm not anymore.

Bonjour, Tristesse

I am flunking out of French
and it's not all *ooh la la*
and *oui, oui, oui,*
it's pretty much all
oh merde and *au revoir.*
Here's what I want to know:
how am I supposed
to speak a foreign tongue
when I've never even seen
another state?
How am I supposed to know
about everywhere else
when I can barely even
navigate my way
around here?

Good Girl

For all her noise about how she hates it here,
next year my sister is going to a college
only two hours away.
She just got accepted today
so now she has her life mapped out
so now she is a good girl
leaving the rest of us
to go bad.

Winter

Winter is upon us
and ice is everywhere,
especially in our living room
where my dad and Susan sit
barely speaking.
Something has happened between them
and I don't know what it is
but I can tell already
it won't melt away.
Seasons come and seasons go
and I'm going to have to say goodbye
to another one.

Gossip

Sometimes I imagine I'm talking to my mother
and when we've exhausted
the secrets of other girls,
I tell her the gossip of my own life:
how Tara gave Bobby to me
without even knowing it,
how Jenny Arnold barely talks to me anymore,
how there's talk of putting Denise in an institution
how I think I love Bobby but maybe
it's just that I can't seem to stop thinking
about Randall Faber's final day in the rain.
I imagine I'm talking to my mother
and somehow it's making it all better
because she's holding my hand
as we sit together on the sofa,
the dogs panting at our feet
and some sweet thing
burning in the oven.

The Way Love Goes

I wake up in the middle of the night
to the sound of someone crying.
I go into Spencer's room
and even though he's fourteen
and almost grown up
I find him curled like a kitten
in a ball at the end of his bed
all soft and sweet and young.
I ask him what's wrong
and he says our parents don't like each other anymore.
How do you know? I say and he says,
Because your dad ate a steak for dinner
and he didn't even care that it made her cry.
I try to tell him this is the way love goes,
it is fluid like tides or weather,
just when it seems like it's going away,
it comes back
and even if it doesn't, that's okay.
Finally he looks at me and says
Is that the way it is with us?
and I tell him he's an idiot and a goofball
and I will always be his stepsister
and I will always love him
and because it's the only way I know

I bring him my globe
and say *If you ever need me*
I'll always be somewhere on this
and I stroke his hair
until he sleeps again.

Two days before Denise burns her house down,
I have a dream I'm hovering above the town.
I see patches of snow on the land,
I see our house and Denise just outside it
one hand on her lighter,
one foot out the door.
I see my father,
knee-deep in the sand
of his half-finished garage
and my stepmother,
fleeing the kitchen,
crackers growing stale in the cupboards,
the cheese molding into hard curls
like my hair in seventh grade.
I see my father and Susan collide in the hallway,
wrap around each other like vines.
From up above the land
I see them crawl and cycle
towards the bedroom,
Susan's cheeks as red
as the ointment
she once slathered
on my stepbrother's scraped knee.
They duck under a beam

and they are lost to me.
I am left hovering up above
my own house,
bits of hunger falling
out of my hands,
spinning to the ground and
landing like ash on the snow.

Things They Taught Me

Like my mother,
I want to stand still
so I can run fast.

Like my sister,
I want to get smart
so I can fail tests.

I want to plant flowers
so I can pull weeds.

I want to make friends
so I can have enemies

I want to fall in love
so I can break hearts.

I want to learn stick shift
so I can drive away from here.

I want to learn to put things on paper
just so I can watch them burn.

I want to grow up
so I can forget this.

6

the Wrong
road Out of town

Away

After they take Denise away
to the hospital
and say it isn't as bad
as it sounds,
I call Bobby.
Come and get me, I say,
and take me away from here,
take me as far away
as you can imagine
going.

Goody-Goody

I may think I'm a badass
but before I leave,
I tape a note to the fridge.
(*Be home soon. Love, Penny*)
As the road ticks by beneath
our secondhand tires,
I berate myself:
How can I be expected
to go somewhere real
and do something great and
be someone wonderful
if I'm still the kind of goody-goody
who leaves a note?

Fun

I wake up and we're on a highway
one and a half states away
from everyone I've ever known.
Bobby makes a joke about
how maybe we should
rob a Quickie Mart for fun.
I don't answer, instead I think how
I feel farther off the map of my life
than I've ever felt.
But wherever I am,
I surely must be closer to my mother,
at least that's what I tell myself.

The Hand of Kentucky

I was the darling girl with chapped lips,
the one wearing her mother's shoes,
savvy with drink.
I was holding Bobby's hand
when his compass needle slid towards Kentucky
like a thief in a dank-water town,
the bluegrass, the racetrack
too bright now for him to ignore.
I've always loved Bobby despite my sister or myself,
despite the smell of garbage around his house
or the bad habits he can't help bringing to bear.
And now Kentucky is like a hand up my skirt,
I can't move towards it or away from it,
I can't say no to Bobby and
his big fist of plans,
so he hitches me in and locks the door tight,
he knows we'll drive until the tip
of Kentucky is three fingers inside me,
he knows that when we cross the state line
Kentucky will have stunned me and won me.
I'll roll my head back against the seat
and moan, the memory of my own hometown
barely even matching
the sweat around my knees.

Rest Stop

Bobby is peeing
and I am looking at the cars fly by,
picturing myself hitching a ride
from a trucker
or better yet,
the Perfect Family.
They could take me in
and love me
like I was their own
until one day
I'm grown and wise and tall
and famous for saying smart things
and then I could go back
to my hometown
and all the people I loved
would be there
alive and bright and well
all the stars lined up
in exact constellations
the way they were made to be.

We stop at a roadside bar in Arizona
because Bobby is the only person in the world
who has gotten lost trying to find the Grand Canyon
but once we're inside,
he forgets about asking directions
and immediately he drinks too much
and talks too much
and the bartender pulls me aside
and asks me if my parents know where I am.
I realize I am on my way to becoming
just another teenage runaway statistic
and I am with a boy who thinks
playing twenty U2 songs in a row on the jukebox
makes him cool.
If Jenny were here
she'd say what would *really* be cool
is to play Merle Haggard
like the locals do.
But I'm not with Jenny, I am with a boy
who is making an ass of himself
and I'm wondering why being here
doesn't feel like
I ever dreamed it would.

Watching Bobby, I realize
the thing about a guy you've
spent your whole life loving from afar
is that even though he's real
you've really made most of him up.

That's probably why I hate *Sleepless in Seattle.*
My stepmom thinks it's romantic
but what she doesn't realize
is that Meg Ryan and Tom Hanks
have done so much fantasizing about each
   other
that if they were in the real world,
getting together would
definitely be a disappointment.
What if you were imagining Tom Cruise
and you got Tom Hanks?
Or what if you were imagining Tom Hanks
and you got Tom Arnold?

Say what you like, but here now,
looking across the room at the boy
I thought I so-called loved,
I am living proof that

a good imagination may be
the best friend of loners
but it is definitely
the enemy of lovers.

How My Mother Felt

Sitting on a gin-soaked stool,
watching the locals drink themselves silly
I wonder if my mother ever felt the way I do:
so proud of herself for getting away
that she couldn't understand
why all she thought about
was going back.

As the eighteenth U2 song plays
(we've heard this one twice now),
Bobby sidles up to me
and slurs, *How about robbing that Quickie Mart?*
I stare at him. *You're joking.*
C'mon, Penny. He gives me a drunk smirk.
Your sister would do it.

Head bowed, I'm on my knees
in front of what feels like thousands.
I'm being arrested for driving the getaway car,
I'm telling my story a mile a minute.
When I finally stand up and
crawl into the cab of the waiting cop car,
pieces of gravel cling to my kneecaps.
I'm not nose-job beautiful
but attractive enough to know
people are looking my way;
I'm no brain surgeon but I know enough
to point the finger at Bobby,
whose idea of dinner is a pint of peach schnapps,
whose mouth had been wooing my collarbone
all night, urgent as bees to a begonia.
Bobby's the one with the bright idea
of robbing the Quick Western Grocery,
Bobby's the guy who got us to where we are now,
some faraway county's tin can police station.
My fingertips are touched with black,
I make my mark on a white card
and on the forearm of Officer Ron,
who I touch long enough to say,
Can't we talk?
When he says no, there are traces of black

along my cheeks and neck,
places my fingers don't remember touching.
I sit there and try to imagine myself miles away
from where the whole stink started,
my knees so tired from kneeling
that I forget the time when all they were good for
was casually holding me upright
and always pointing out the place
my skirt should never touch.

C'mon, Penny. Snap out of it. Whadya say?

My little imaginary Robbing-The-Quickie-Mart fantasy is
over and Bobby's still standing right where I left him,
smirking away. *You know your sister would do it.*

I'm not my sister, I say. I look at him standing there,
and then I speak three words I never in my life thought
I'd utter to Bobby Lanegan: *Take me home.*

Huh? He stares at me.

Right now.

He burps. *What's gotten into you?*

Some sense, I say and turn and walk to the door.

When it opens, the light hits me in the face,
giving me a little slap like the ones
you sometimes see a mean mom giving her kid,
a little slap that says some dark red dreams
are meant not to sleep in for long
and now is the time
to wake out of this one.

7

the flanks of home

Over Now

Bobby doesn't say much on the drive home
which is okay.
I can tell by the look on his face
he knows like I do
that our love, if you could even call it that,
wasn't meant to live long,
it had a short lifespan from the start
the way certain things do
that are born one season
and are dead by the next.

Premature and underweight, our love was born in
   winter.
Once it was born, it grew up fast.
It was crawling one day and walking the next,
sucking a tit during breakfast, getting teeth by
   lunchtime.
Pretty soon, it started sneaking out at night.
The police would find it lying in someone's yard,
staring up at the stars.

One day we left it with a sitter
and when we got home, the sitter was gone
and our love was in the living room,
calling all its friends.
The next day we took it to the doctor,
who said it had a disease.
It couldn't live in a regular house,
it could never have a normal life.
Our love, he said, wouldn't last the winter.

It is spring now and our love has been laid to rest.
Even though I'm advised against it
I can't help thinking about its short little life—
how its first word was *you* and its last was *me*,
how it would come home drunk after a dance,

how it learned to swim in only an afternoon,
how the two of us stood at the edge
of the community pool, cheering it on,
amazed that such a clumsy creature
could even begin to float.

Phone Call Home

When we get to the ferry,
I call my father.
He doesn't say much,
just that he'll pick me up
at the ferry dock
and if he sees Bobby anywhere near me,
he'll shoot him,
he swears to God,
he will.

The Thing About Boats

This is the thing about boats.
You meet people out there
on the water
that you never normally would
on land.

People on boats
are usually
swimming between one place
and another,
the past or the future,
this body of land
or that one.

Being at sea
is being somewhere
in the middle of things.
Being at sea
is being everywhere
and nowhere
all at once.

Marlene

I was on my way back home when I met Marlene.
She turned to me on the ferry boat,
a stranger of foreign proportions,
somebody's out-of-town guest.
Isn't it beautiful here? she said.
I'd had so much beauty in my life
I was practically hungover from it.
The sea, looking like lava and spittle,
careened out behind us.
Marlene went on to say she was recovering
from Iowa and alcoholism,
and I noted that she was too doped-up on salt water
to think straight.
I could get used to a place like this,
she said, and I told her how it was:
the deer you kill just driving into town,
the rain that ruins your birthday parties,
the mothers who become your ex-mothers
almost immediately after you can walk.
Marlene didn't seem to care;
she wore a charmed smile,
a dubious track record,
and she was high on the promise of the place.
Look out there, she said,
grabbing one of my tired arms

and spinning me west.
With my pupils smaller
than they had been in months,
she pointed out
that the sea, on this summer day,
was a blanket of light
and that she, Marlene, was ready
to have her days filled with light like that.
I stood beside her,
a little changed and unchanged,
barely even caring that my cheeks were getting burned,
that my hair was tangling itself beyond extraction
into hers.

Home to the Pocket

I leap rivers and mountains,
I float across the platter of night
to reach my house, the other state
still fresh on my hands.
I've only been gone four days
but when I arrive, my father hugs me hard
and my sister tells me I'm a jerk
and my stepmother is gasping like a fish,
from panic and maybe liquor, and I am
back in the pocket,
sixteen and still my father's girl,
the sweet hard star of his hand
upon mine, the wide planks of sky
filling my eye.

By the time I get home, I've been grounded for two months and my sister has already found out where I've been and with whom.

I could have warned you about him, but you wouldn't have listened to me anyway, she says.

Yes, I would have, I say, not sure if I mean it.

Are you kidding? You're too busy being <u>you</u> to ever listen to <u>me</u>.

I stare at her.

How could she not know that all I ever wanted was to listen to her stupid warnings? How could she not know that I was desperate for every tall tale she had to tell? How come families are full of people that have no clue how they make each other feel?

Radio Silence

I called Jenny today
and told her I miss her.
She said, *It's about time, you big lame-ass*
and then made me promise
that the second
I'm un-grounded,
we're going record shopping.

As for my stepbrother,
he hasn't said one word to me
since I got home.

Tacos

Last night I sat down next to Spencer
and watched an entire episode
of *Star Trek* with him
and when it was over,
I said, *That was good*
and he got up and left the room
like I wasn't ever even there.

So tonight, after I found my globe
sitting on my bed
with a note from him that said,
I don't want this anymore,
I went to the kitchen and
made him our favorite food
and went into his room
handed him seven tacos on a plate
and walked out.

All I can think
is that if he doesn't want me back now,
he never will.

The Thing About Telescopes

The stars are out in full bloom tonight,
so while everyone sleeps,
I bring my dad's telescope out of the garage
and point it up to the sky.

What they don't tell you about telescopes, though,
is that they make your eyes hurt
from the squint and the strain
and that no matter how much you adjust and focus,
it's still hard to see the stars
you came out there to see.

Maybe telescopes weren't made to bring you closer
to what's up there, after all.
Maybe telescopes were made to help you realize
that the stars will always be far away
and maybe that's part
of what makes them so beautiful.

Bacon and Eggs

When I get up the next morning,
Susan has mock-scrambled-eggs
and Fakin' Bacon waiting for me,
and she says she got Dad to agree
I could go see Denise.
Then she tells me that
she ran away once
when she was a girl,
but it was for three weeks
not just three days.
It's funny—I never imagined
my stepmother as a "girl" before,
only as the lady
who moved into my house
without asking,
but I guess everyone's
got another version of themselves
living inside them,
you just don't get to see it
all the time.

Susan drops me off at the visitor's center
and tells me she'll be back in half an hour.
It's weird but I kind of want her to stay
because I have no idea what my best friend
is going to be like or act like
but then after a few minutes
out walks Denise.

I can't say she looks great
but she doesn't look awful,
she's just not a whole lot
like the girl I grew up with,
but then again, she'd bagged and buried
that version of herself
a long time ago.

As she walks towards me,
I realize maybe sometimes things aren't meant
to go back to what they were before,
and as Denise hugs me hello,
it's a new thing and an old one
and that's just how it is
and it's good.

Dear Denise

After we get home, I stand out in the yard
watching the rain bear down on our hometown.
I imagine you not in the hospital but instead
in Mexico, climbing the pyramids
and living to tell about it.
I imagine your sunburn is deepening, its pink landscape
spreading across your arms and shoulders.
You are taking to the pyramids on all fours,
overdosing on that great, triangular height.
I think of you nearing the top,
the way those ancient stones must feel,
the atoms of heat tittering around you.
I imagine you opening yourself up to the world,
to storms and pyramids,
to all these small, immaculate dangers
that make up our lives.

Home Safe

Tonight is my dad's birthday and
Susan made turkey spaghetti
(somewhere between a vegan
and red meat meal).

When we all sit down,
my dad holds up his mug of beer
and makes a toast, something mushy
about how he loves us all
and he always will
and he's glad we're all home safe.

Then he gets up and goes around the table
and kisses Susan full on the mouth
and dips her like they're on the dance floor
and my sister says, *People! Please!*
Spencer and I crack up
and he gives me the tiniest little smile.

How we all came together,
I have no idea, but however it did,
it happened,
like a miracle of science,
of chemistry or biology,
we came together
and we stayed.

A new guy moved into our neighborhood
and my sister says I can have him.
He's too young for her
even though he's cute.
I see him outside his house doing chores
today when I'm walking the dogs
down to the beach.
She was right.
He is cute.
Cuter than cute.
He gives me a wave and
my heart thumps
and I start imagining
everything that could happen;
our whole story unfolds
in four seconds flat.
Isn't it strange the places on the map
your heart can take you?
And then you figure out
sometimes it's okay to stay still for a while,
you don't have to go everywhere all at once,
you can see a boy
and you can love him for a minute
and maybe it's real and maybe it's not

but sometimes all you have to do is
wave back and
keep going.

I keep going
all the way down to the shoreline.
You'd think the dogs would love it here,
the way the salt kisses the stones,
but something scares them
about the way the waves
recede and return
out and back in again.

I take my mother's globe
out of my backpack,
the globe that's been given from her to me
and from me to my stepbrother
and now back to me again.
I take aim and throw it out into the sea
and it seems like for a second
the dogs might swim after it
but they don't.

I stand there watching it
and after a while it starts drifting out
farther and farther and I know now
I'll never see her again
and it took me a while to figure out

that's not good or bad
it's just the way
it is.

On My Arm

I am back in my hometown. I am eating biscuits at the café, I'm writing a novel on my arm. This is the first part of Chapter 1, near my wrist. On the way to breakfast, I see a white horse, its knees buckling into the pasture. It's summer again and the clamor for shellfish is on; the tide's out and birds and businessmen both are up to their elbows in sand. It's so postcard-perfect here that I'm building a tolerance for beauty. Things I hate, like bird shit and link sausage, flatbed trucks and tattooed forearms, even they seem charmed. At the beach, as the gulls get luckier than the grocers, I think of the white horse fallen down, the fingers of water that manage to poke their way into everything, my little life on its tiny plate, with a side dish of sky and a spoon to go with it.

Wonderful

I don't even bother knocking on my stepbrother's door,
I just barge in and pull him off his bed
and say, *You're coming with me.*

All the way down to the docks,
he won't talk to me
but that's okay because I shove him in the dinghy
and I say, *Row* and he does.

We take turns rowing
until we are in the center of the bay
and I say that I'm sorry for leaving him like that
but sometimes you have to do stupid things
to swim your way back into the smart ones.

After a second, he says, *Fine. I forgive you.*
I look at his often-annoying face
and I lean over and whisper
into his mostly dirty ears
the first of many stupid warnings
and tall tales that I plan to
spend his life telling him.

I guess if you look at it
I'm right where I started

and everything is still trees and water and rain
and small town, small town,
but no matter how you slice it,
it is my life
and I am floating right out here
in the middle of it.

Jason Lust

Kirsten Smith is the cowriter of the feature films *Legally Blonde, 10 Things I Hate About You, Ella Enchanted,* and *She's the Man.* Her award-winning poetry has appeared in such literary journals as *The Gettysburg Review, Witness, Massachusetts Review,* and *Prairie Schooner.* She lives in Los Angeles, where she likes going to rock shows and hanging out with her dogs. Her Web site is www.kiwilovesyou.com.

acknowledgments

The author gratefully acknowledges the following publications in which several poems in this book have previously appeared: *Hayden's Ferry Review, Left Bank, The Massachusetts Review, North Dakota Quarterly, On the Bus, Rush Hour, Shenandoah, Soundings East,* and *Witness.*

Utmost love and gratitude to Mel and Katie Aline, best friends, beautiful parents and purveyors of the finest writer's colony on the West Coast. Infinite thanks to Susan Phillips, the best teacher I've ever had. Thank you to Steven Malk, punk rock agent extraordinaire, for inspiring this endeavor; Megan Tingley for her belief in the book; and Amy Hsu for her wonderful and precise guidance. To Ryan Latimer, Gregory McCracken, Stacey Lutz, and Micah Rafferty for their collegiate encouragement, when it was most needed. To Catalaine Knell, for always reminding me I am a poet. To Seth Jaret for his enthusiasm and creativity. Love and kisses to Noel Krueger for being the girl I've always looked up to. Many thanks to Shannon Woodward for lending her foxiness to the cover of this book. To Brandon McWhorter for his creativity. To Elwood Reid and Doug Cooney for their inspirational work and wisdom. Thanks to The MacDowell Colony, who provided the picnic lunches that fortified many of these poems. To Shauna Cross for her witty prose. To Alene Moroni, Michael Hacker, and Doug Wyman for their constant and true friendship. Thank you, Lusty, for being such a drama king. And thanks to the movies, Madonna, and Courtney Love, all of whom inspired me to leave town and then come back again.